D0365162

First American Edition.
Copyright © 1999 Disney Enterprises, Inc.
All rights reserved under international copyright conventions.
Published in the United States by Grolier Books, a division of Grolier Enterprises, Inc. Originally published in Denmark by Egmont Gruppen, Copenhagen.

ISBN: 0-7172-8965-6

Manufactured in the United States of America.
A B C D 1 2 3 4

Walt Disney's

Mickey and the Beanstalk

GROLIER BOOKS

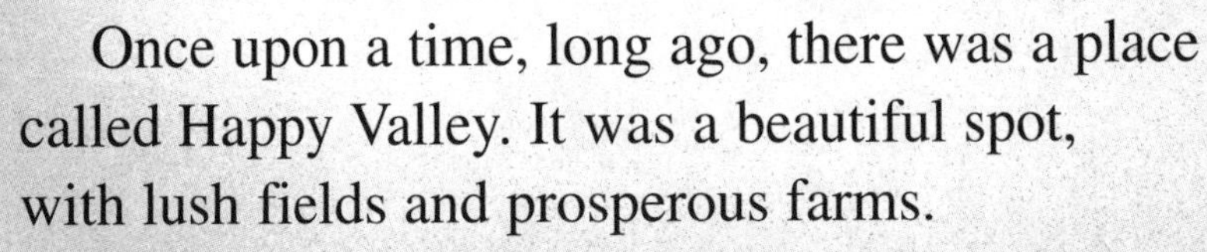

Once upon a time, long ago, there was a place called Happy Valley. It was a beautiful spot, with lush fields and prosperous farms.

High above the green valley stood a shining castle, where a magical singing harp lived. This golden harp had an enchanted voice. When she sang, she cast a wondrous spell of peace and joy over the valley.

One day something terrible happened. A mysterious shadow crept over the valley. When the shadow lifted, the golden harp was gone!

Without the enchantment of the harp, Happy Valley was no longer happy. Everything dried up. Everyone became miserable.

Days passed, weeks passed, and things only got worse.

In a small, run-down cabin lived three farmers. They were three very *hungry* farmers, for their crops did not grow. They had no money and no food, only an old cow.

The farmers' names were Mickey, Goofy, and Donald. They sat down to share their last meal—one slice of bread and one single bean.

"Hey, fellas!" Mickey eagerly cried. "I know! Let's sell the cow and buy something to eat!" It was a good idea. So Mickey took the cow into town. Donald and Goofy waited, dreaming of hot, delicious food.

Mickey soon returned home.

"What did you get?" the two asked excitedly. "Turkey? Lobster? Sweet potato pie?"

"Beans!" announced Mickey.

"Beans?!" yelled Donald.

"Yes, but not ordinary beans," Mickey explained. "These are *magic* beans."

"Do you know what you get if you plant magic beans by the light of a full moon?" Mickey cheerfully asked.

"Yeah, more beans!" Donald answered angrily, knocking them out of Mickey's hands.

Poor Mickey! Someone had talked him into trading his cow for three magic beans. What a mean trick!

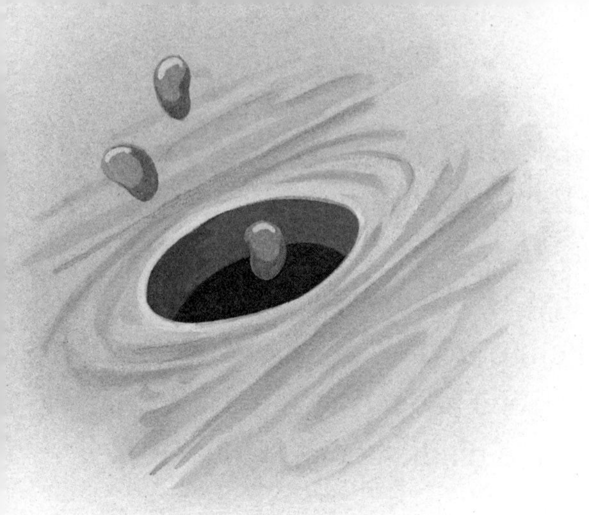

The beans fell to the floor and rolled into a hole.

That night, after bedtime, something strange happened. By the light of the full moon, the beans began to grow. And grow. And grow!

Higher and higher, all through the night, they grew into a giant beanstalk. The great stalk lifted the little house up into the sky!

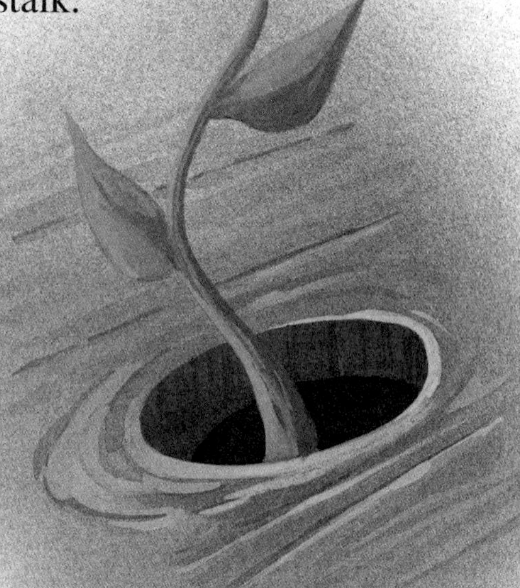

The next morning, the farmers awoke miles above the earth. A fantastic new world surrounded them.

"Hey, fellas!" Goofy yelled, pointing. "Look over there!"

They turned to see a giant castle. Who lived there? The curious friends set off to find out.

"Ouch!" yelped Goofy, falling into a big hole.

"Hey, watch where you're falling!" scolded Donald, stepping on Goofy's head.

The three explorers did not notice that the hole was really a footprint, made by a giant foot!

They soon reached the castle.
"Gawrsh, it's awful big!" said Goofy.
It *was* big. The biggest castle anyone had ever seen. They had to climb on top of one another to get up the huge steps.

The brave farmers soon reached the massive door. What was inside? What mystery lurked within the dark walls?

"Uh, anybody home?" Mickey asked nervously, knocking on the door.

There was no answer. Bravely, they crawled under the door and entered the castle.

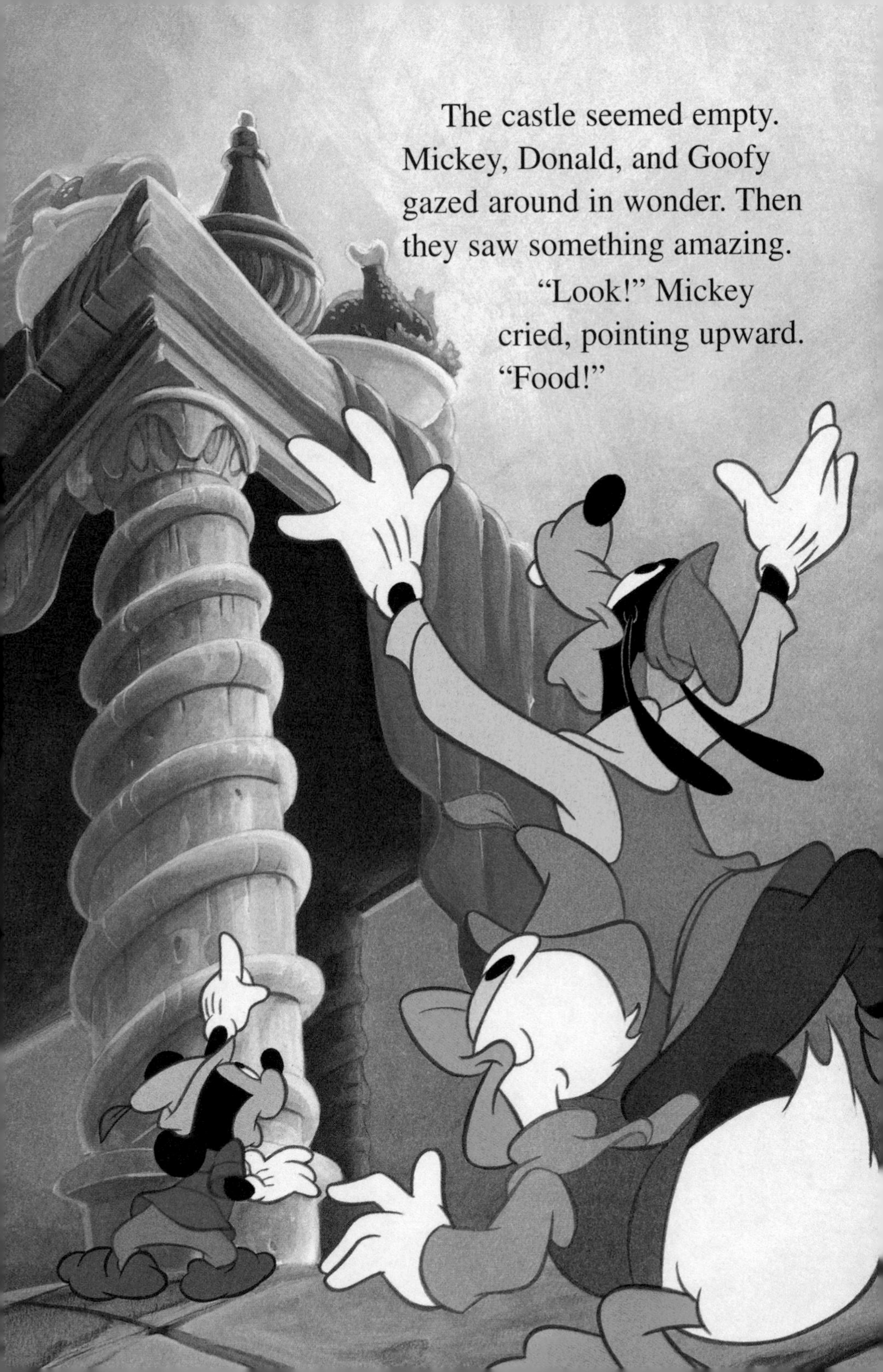

The castle seemed empty. Mickey, Donald, and Goofy gazed around in wonder. Then they saw something amazing.

"Look!" Mickey cried, pointing upward. "Food!"

And *what* food! Peas the size of tennis balls! Cheese as big as a house! A drumstick larger than twenty chickens!

The hungry farmers devoured the tasty treats.

"Hello!" called a familiar voice. "Is anyone there?"

The sound came from a locked box.

"It's the magic harp!" Mickey said, looking inside. "How did you get here?"

"I was kidnapped by that awful giant!" replied the harp.

Giant? Yes, it was true. The three friends were in the home of a giant named Willy! He was a magical giant who could change his shape into anything he wanted.

Mighty footsteps boomed through the castle. The giant was coming!

"FE-FI-FO-FUM!" bellowed the giant. "I smell—"

Oh no! Did he smell Mickey, Goofy, or Donald? "I smell pot roast!" the giant roared. "Chocolate pot roast with green gravy. Yum!"

The hungry giant ate. He did not see the frightened farmers hiding on his table!

The giant made himself a sandwich. He took two slices of bread … cut a chunk of cheese … put in some meat … added pepper and …

"Ah … ah … ah-choo!"

Mickey popped out of the sandwich!

"Ha, ha! Gesundheit!" laughed Mickey nervously.

But Willy wasn't laughing. Mickey had to think fast. So he came up with a plan to trick the giant.

"Is it true that you're magical and can change yourself into anything?" asked Mickey.

"Sure!" Willy replied. "You want to see? Name something. Anything."

"Okay," Mickey answered. "A housefly."

Mickey, Goofy, and Donald found a flyswatter. They planned to swat Willy when he turned into a fly!

But Willy did not turn into a housefly. He turned into a big, pink bunny with long ears!

"Hey, you tried to trick me!" the angry giant realized.

Willy changed back into a giant. He caught all three of the tricksters in one hand.

As the giant dropped them into the box with the harp, Mickey escaped. Willy locked the box and put the key in his pocket.

“I have to save the others!” Mickey said, “but how?”

Luckily, the magic harp knew what to do. She sang a soft, sweet lullaby and slowly, gently, Willy began to nod off.

"Oh, boy!" Mickey soon whispered. "He's asleep!"

Quietly, Mickey climbed down to the sleeping giant. He was going to get the key and unlock the prisoners.

But the giant's pocket was full of dust. It tickled Mickey's nose and made him sneeze!

"Ah ... ah ... ah-choo!"

"Hey, what was that?" Willy wondered, waking up.

But Mickey was fast. Quick as a flash, he climbed up and away with the key. Willy never noticed. He went back to sleep.

“You did it!” Donald cheered happily as Mickey unlocked the box.

“Let’s get out of here before the giant wakes up!” Mickey cried.

So Donald and Goofy picked up the harp and headed for the door.

"Wait a minute," Mickey added. "I've got an idea."

He wanted to make doubly sure that the giant would not follow them. So he started to tie Willy's shoelaces together.

But the plan backfired. Willy woke up!

“Come back here!” the giant shouted furiously, chasing after them.

Donald and Goofy were already hurrying down the beanstalk with the magic harp. Mickey followed, flying on a popped cork!

“You can’t get away from Willy!” bellowed the mad monster. He rushed down the beanstalk after Mickey.

Meanwhile, Donald and Goofy had reached the bottom. They quickly found a big saw. Working together, the speedy pair soon cut the beanstalk down.

“Uh, oh,” said Willy nervously.
He was helpless. Down he tumbled, over and over. Down and down, he fell and fell to another place far, far away.

The magic harp returned to Happy Valley. The valley once again became beautiful and green. It echoed with song and laughter. Peace and prosperity reigned.

Mickey, Donald, and Goofy were joyful. Their crops grew again. They were no longer poor and hungry. Everyone in Happy Valley lived happily ever after.